CW01090964

SPRING

A SURREAL STORIES COLLECTION

DEAN WESLEY SMITH

PUBLISHING

ALSO BY DEAN WESLEY SMITH

COLD POKER GANG

Kill Game

Cold Call

Calling Dead

Bad Beat

Dead Hand

Freezeout

Ace High

Burn Card

Heads Up

Ring Game

Bottom Pair

Case Card

THE POKER BOY UNIVERSE

Poker Boy

The Slots of Saturn: A Poker Boy Novel

They're Back: A Poker Boy Short Novel

Luck Be Ladies: A Poker Boy Collection

Playing a Hunch: A Poker Boy Collection

A Poker Boy Christmas: A Poker Boy Collection

Ghost of a Chance

The Poker Chip: A Ghost of a Chance Novel

The Christmas Gift: A Ghost of a Chance Novel

The Free Meal: A Ghost of a Chance Novel

The Cop Car: A Ghost of a Chance Novella

The Deep Sunset: A Ghost of a Chance Novel

Marble Grant

The First Year: A Marble Grant Novel

Time for Cool Madness: Six Crazy Marble Grant Stories

Pakhet Jones

The Big Tom: A Packet Jones Short Novel

Big Eyes: A Packet Jones Short Novel

THUNDER MOUNTAIN

Thunder Mountain

Monumental Summit

Avalanche Creek

The Edwards Mansion

Lake Roosevelt

Warm Springs

Melody Ridge

Grapevine Springs

The Idanha Hotel

The Taft Ranch

Tombstone Canyon

Dry Creek Crossing

Hot Springs Meadow

Green Valley

SEEDERS UNIVERSE

Dust and Kisses: A Seeders Universe Prequel Novel

Against Time

Sector Justice

Morning Song

The High Edge

Star Mist

Star Rain

Star Fall

Starburst

Rescue Two

CONTENTS

Introduction   xi
It All Might Be Seasonable

The Park, the Yard, and Other Cold Places   1
For The Show Of It   13
The Stone Slept Here   25
It's My Party   37
Wings Out   47
Stranger in the Shadows   61
Something in My Darling   75
Remembering the Last Laugh   85
The Man Who Laughed on a Rainy Night   97
Why Delay? Just Rub   109

Newsletter sign-up   121
About the Author   123
Expanded Copyright Information   125

SPRING

INTRODUCTION

IT ALL MIGHT BE SEASONABLE

For years and years, actually decades and decades, I kept saying that one day I would do a Bryant Street collection or two, and I just never got around to it.

Finally, in the winter of 2023, I decided it was time and told the fine folks at WMG Publishing I was going to do this. Stephanie Writt came up with the cool street-sign logo and I was off.

I thought it would be cool to have Bryant Street be a television series with four seasons of ten episodes each season. (For those of you who don't know, a short story usually has enough story for a single thirty-minute episode of anything on television.)

So I sent the idea of four seasons to Stephanie at WMG and back comes the four wonderful covers using seasons of the year. I was about to object when it dawned on me that four seasons of the year would be a lot easier to explain than four seasons of a television show.

And these would act as ten episodes of a season, but each season would start on the first day of the named season. A full year of Bryant Street.

So I started with the forty stories together and then put them into seasons.

Often a story is set in the title season. Or the story is dark like winter. Or hot like summer.

Or a character in the last days of their lives like winter, or fading like fall. In one way or another, all the stories fit into a season.

But think of them like ten episodes per run. The winter season run, the spring season run, and so on.

Sort of like ten episodes per season of a series like *The Twilight Zone* television series used to be. Every episode different, yet every episode set on Bryant Street.

Smith's
STORIES

DEAN WESLEY SMITH
THE PARK, THE YARD,
AND OTHER COLD PLACES
A Bryant Street Story

THE PARK, THE YARD, AND OTHER COLD PLACES

Bobby Liebert killed his wife. He had his reasons. And he had planned everything right down to the last detail.

Only detail he forgot to take into account was that he lived on Bryant Street.

———

Bobbie Liebert killed his wife, Stephanie, on the afternoon of April sixth in the spare bedroom, second one down the hall, of their three-bedroom ranch house on Bryant Street.

He told her he was painting the room because she had always complained that the robin's egg light blue wasn't the best color for her sewing room. So he promised to paint it and three years went by before one Friday evening he finally moved all of her stuff out into the other bedroom, which had become her reading room, covered the shag

1

carpet with a large painting tarp, made sure she had approved the color, and then killed her in that room, on the painting tarp.

He used a hammer to the back of the head and managed to keep the bleeding on the tarp.

He no longer loved her and she clearly no longer loved him. And just killing her seemed so much easier than divorce and still having her around in the same city.

His plan was simple. Kill her and bury her in the park down the street.

Bobbie was a short man at five-three and identified with being short. His suits were always perfect and he had three of them in his closet, all identical brown. He owned five different ties that went with the suits, one for each day of the week.

He ate the same Frosted Flakes every morning for breakfast, the same peanut butter and honey and lunchmeat sandwich every lunch, and often brought home dinner from a Chinese restaurant or Kentucky Fried Chicken depending on the day of the week.

He carefully planned everything every day. Including killing Stephanie.

Stephanie hadn't worked a day since they got married. She did a lot of sewing and also said she hoped to be a writer, but had a lot of reading to do first.

The first couple of years of the marriage, Bobbie didn't mind at all. His job as a manager of a major grocery store paid them enough money to live in the nice house on Bryant Street. Buy food and clothes and put some away.

And they only needed one car, so they lived within their means just fine.

But five years into the marriage, when he suggested she go to school to learn how to write, she didn't speak with him for months.

Actually it had been a relief because she talked all the time about nothing and Bobbie loved his quiet more than anything.

Everything about the marriage just got worse.

She was asleep when he went to bed and still asleep when he got up and left for work. And when they were together over dinners, all she did was talk and nag and talk, usually about nothing.

And Bobbie was a problem solver, so he solved his Stephanie problem and just killed her.

Very, very simple. Now he just had to bury her.

He pulled his SUV into the garage, made sure the garage door was down, and after wrapping Stephanie up in the tarp, he dragged her to the car and lifted her into the back. Thankfully, she had stayed as light as when they had first got married. She was taller than he was, but very skinny.

He went back into the house, cleaned up his hammer as best he could and hung it back in the garage. Then he moved the furniture back into her sewing room. He didn't bother to paint over the robin's egg blue. He kind of liked the color, actually.

Then around one in the morning, with a shovel in the back seat and Stephanie all the way in the back, wrapped up, he drove down Bryant Street to the neighborhood park called the Bryant Street Park.

It was about five square blocks and took up the center of the subdivision. It had a few tennis courts, a playground for the kids, and a lot of grass and old oak trees. Park benches and picnic tables were scattered in different locations under the trees.

Bryant Street ran along the west side and Stephanie had always commented how beautiful the place was. Every single time they drove by, didn't matter the season.

But heaven forbid they should ever stop. Take a walk. Enjoy the beauty.

"Later," she would always say. After a few years he had stopped suggesting it.

Seems like now was later. At least for her.

He pulled off the road near a group of tall old oak trees just getting their spring leaves. Houses across the street from the park were dark.

He took the shovel and a fresh painter's tarp and walked back into the park, looking for a place to silently dig a grave for Stephanie that was dark enough that he wouldn't be heard or seen.

She had never wanted to stop here, but if he had his way, she would soon exist here a long time.

He found a perfect place about ten paces beyond a big oak, far enough away to not be troubled by the roots.

He carefully cut out a rectangle from the sod, putting it on one side of the tarp in the exact way he had taken it out. He wanted to return it in a way that it wouldn't be seen.

Then as quietly as he could, he started digging in the soft, moist soil. He was used to work, lifting boxes and such at the store, and he knew this would be work, so he went slowly, letting the hole get deeper and each shovel-full of dirt carefully piled on the tarp.

It was going fine until about two feet down he ran into a painter's tarp.

And when he got down and felt around in the hole, it quickly became apparent that there was already a body buried there.

And it had a pretty nasty odor to it.

So he quickly filled back in the hole and then put the sod back. He had been tempted to leave the hole open, but he knew his prints might be all over the tarp he had put the dirt on.

He folded up his dirt tarp and went looking for another location.

One spot looked perfect, about twenty paces from a picnic table and beside a row of bushes.

So once again he laid the tarp down, carefully removed the grass sod, and started digging. Again, down about three feet this time there was a body, this one of a woman in house dress, no tarp covering her. And she had been dead for some time.

Bobbie just couldn't believe his luck.

Was there a body under every perfect spot in this entire park?

So once again he filled back in the hole, put the sod back in place, folded up his tarp and headed for the car. He was going to need to get Stephanie into their big freezer in the garage, so she didn't start smelling, and himself cleaned up and to bed. The sun would be coming up in an hour.

He got everything cleaned up and Stephanie in the freezer that they never used and hadn't used even though Stephanie had thought it would be a great thing to have.

He woke up the next morning at around eleven a.m., Saturday, with the sounds of a neighbor's mower.

And no sounds of Stephanie snoring.

He turned on some light jazz, something that Stephanie would have never allowed, had a wonderfully quiet breakfast, then went out and looked into the freezer.

"Morning, dear," he said to the curled-up corpse still wrapped in a painting tarp.

He took stock of how much room was in the freezer, then headed to his own store to check in on how the Saturday crew was doing and to buy some meat.

"Stocking up my freezer," he told his assistant manager, then got all the meat home and covering Stephanie's body. It looked like a very well-stocked freezer when he was done. No sign of anything in a painting tarp under the meat.

He thought about just leaving her there, then decided he really felt he needed to bury her.

So Sunday afternoon, after another wonderful night's sleep, he headed out into his own backyard where the previous owners used to have a garden and started to work on it. He would never actually plant a garden. Didn't interest him, but he needed to have his neighbors think he was going to.

He got down about four feet when he found another body. This one of a woman about Stephanie's age, wrapped in a tarp almost identical to the one he had her frozen in.

The buried woman had been buried long enough that most of the smell was gone, so he opened the tarp just a little and looked at her. She had been beautiful, he could tell that much.

He closed the tarp back up and quickly replaced the dirt, making sure that it looked like he was about to plant a garden in the freshly moved soil by the time he was done. Right down to digging rows and everything.

Then he headed back inside, stored the shovel in the garage and got cleaned up and decided to go out and get KFC and a bag of chips to eat later watching television.

Stephanie would never let him do that.

When he got back, the sun was starting to go down. He just stood on his driveway and looked up and down the street of mostly identical ranch homes, all well-kept.

How many killers like him lived on this street? Clearly more than one. He had killed Stephanie, but not the others. It seemed like such a nice street, on the surface.

And if he found two bodies in the park, how many others were buried there?

And in the backyards of all the homes.

Bryant Street was no doubt a very strange place.

He went inside and put the chips and chicken on the counter and went into Stephanie's sewing room. It was no longer her sewing room, now. He could do with the room as he wanted.

And if anyone asked, which no one would, she had moved back East where her family had been from, but were now all dead.

He got a handcart out of the garage and loaded up her sewing desk and took it to the garage. He put the clean side up of the painting tarp on the top of the freezer and then put the sewing machine desk up on the freezer.

Then he stacked her chair on top of the freezer and a couple boxes of her clothes from the closet so for the first time he would have room for his own clothes.

And over the next few weeks, he had so much stuff stacked in and around the freezer, the big white thing was almost impossible to see.

He had buried Stephanie, just not in the ground, but in her own stuff.

He had tried to bury her in the ground. He really had.

But on Bryant Street, there just wasn't enough room.

Smith's
STORIES

DEAN WESLEY SMITH

FOR THE SHOW OF IT
A Bryant Street Story

FOR THE SHOW OF IT

On Bryant Street, anything seemed possible. Even the magic of a 1966 AMC Rambler Classic car.

Who knew a Rambler held magic.

But just not the kind of divorce magic Les Davis imagined.

————

It was a '66 AMC Rambler Classic 4-Door sedan.

In 2022, those cars didn't exist anymore on the roads. They had pretty much vanished to classic car shows. Even originally it had been an plain-looking brand, never much admired by anyone except a person looking for a cheap family car.

Basic transportation. And they usually came in a pale green, although I remember blue and black ones. But the one I now owned was pale green, now even faded more from all the years and weather.

Ramblers were more a moving box than anything and never thought of as a status symbol. You didn't keep a Rambler if you had enough money to buy a better car.

My name is Les Davis and I didn't care about the history of the car, who bought them originally, and why you never saw one on the road anymore. All I cared about was the fact that it was ugly, in horrid condition, and just almost hurt to look at it.

Perfect.

I spent two hundred bucks for it and then another three hundred to have it put on the back of a flatbed truck from the field where it had been sitting for thirty or forty years, and then dumped in my garage on Bryant Street.

And it was placed so I couldn't really close the door or get another car inside.

There were still weeds growing around the long-flat tires and the rust had taken over a lot of the pale green. Two side windows were broken out and there was a massive dent in the trunk.

Just perfect.

The rules of the Bryant Street subdivision wouldn't allow me to park the old pile of junk in my yard or my driveway, but no rule anywhere said I couldn't have it in my garage, or that I had to close the door.

And if I listened carefully, I could hear the property values dropping through the floor around me. That just makes me laugh since I had come to loathe all my neighbors.

At that moment, my wife Fran pulled up into the driveway in her new Lexus. Now her car fit the status of all the neighbors around us. And she loved being that person who was always just slightly ahead of the neighbors in special things.

She is a beautiful woman who as a top real estate agent in the area, always kept herself up. And that included this house, one of the best on the block, of course.

I owned and ran five sports equipment stores here in town. So my schedule and Fran's schedule lately had had trouble matching. Actually, everything about us as a couple the last few years had trouble matching.

I stood there next to the Rambler with a white T-shirt on that was stained, old Levis, and torn-up tennis shoes.

Fran got out of the car dressed in black heels, a slinky skirt, a silk blouse, and clearly had had her hair done while out for the day. Over the last three years we had drifted so far apart in our drive and values, I no longer really knew her.

Her parents were killed in a plane crash four years ago and ever since we never really could talk. I had tried my best for a year or so, but I had become worthless to her.

There was no doubt she didn't know me anymore either.

We had talked divorce, but she wanted far more of my money from my father's estate than I was willing to give. And she didn't want to leave Bryant Street.

So we had stopped even talking about a divorce.

So in comes the Rambler and a brand new hobby for me.

I honestly had no intention of fixing up a Rambler, but I was going to tell her I did to get her to agree to a decent settlement on the divorce.

Her status on Bryant Street was critical to her. A junk pile of the remains of a Rambler would be a horror for her, especially exposed to the entire street.

She came toward me like she had no intention of stopping before plowing me to the concrete. But stop she did.

"What? Is? That?"

She pointed to the Rambler without really looking at it.

"A 1966 Classic Rambler," I said, pretending to be excited. "You just don't see these cars on the road anymore, so when I saw this one in a field, I had to have it. Always wanted to fix up a classic car and I figured a Classic Rambler would be the one to do."

She opened her mouth, then closed it. Then opened it again, then closed it.

Now Fran was a very attractive woman, usually in total control, but her imitation of a fish didn't help that look.

She turned from me and just stared at the fading green pile of neglect.

Finally she said, "Close the garage door."

"Can't," I said. "It was dumped too far out and this won't be rolling on any wheels for a while I'm afraid."

This time only one fish imitation before she stopped staring at the car and turned and clicked on those high heels into the house.

I patted the dusty old Rambler on the roof and said, "That went well."

Then I headed inside to see what ultimatums she was going to give me that I actually might accept.

I found her in our bedroom already down to her underwear, which I had to admit was a good look on her. Too bad that our troubles also included no sex for as long as I could remember.

She said nothing, but instead dug in a lower drawer and pulled out some old jeans I hadn't seen her in for years and then put on a t-shirt that she had gotten from a 5k charity run.

When she laced up an old pair of sneakers, I had a hunch I was in trouble.

"I've been going to counseling about our marriage," she said.

That shocked me and I might have done a fish imitation before deciding to just let her finish.

"My counselor wants me to try to do things with you, do things together like we used to do."

I nodded.

"I remember telling you that my parents," she said, "when I was growing up, had a green Rambler sedan just like the one you bought."

Okay, fish imitation on strong. Shit! Shit! Shit! She always said I never listened to her. It wasn't that I didn't listen, I just never remembered what she said.

"I told you that I loved that Rambler and how the seats went flat to make a big bed when we went camping."

I had a vague memory of her telling me that kind of story. No memory of it being a Rambler. Shit.

"So I want to help in the restoration," she said, coming toward me. "I miss my parents something awful and this will help me feel close to them again. And to my childhood. And to you, most importantly."

She put her arms around my neck and kissed me, not the peck of long-time married people, but like we used to kiss back in the day.

"So thank you," she said. "I'm sure we're going to bungle the restoration, but it will be fun bungling it together."

And she kissed me again, and this kiss and a push against my leg had a promise of events later in it.

Then she held me slightly away and I could see the bright light in her eyes, the passion that had been gone for so long.

"So what do we do first?" she asked.

Now I did the fish imitation and then laughed. Why not? Not the response I expected, but if working on a pile of junk could save our marriage, I was all in.

"We get a couple of thick notebooks," I said, "and go out and start doing an inventory of all the parts we will need and all the projects that need to be done. And try to put them in order, as best as our limited knowledge will allow us."

She nodded. "I like that."

"And then we start making some calls to people like a mechanic who can get us an engine and a transmission."

"And tire people," she said, "to match the tires from 1966."

"Exactly," I said. "Interior, painters, chrome people, and so on. We are basically the project managers who will get dirty with the cleaning and polishing and smaller stuff and make sure things are on track and done to our standards."

"Our standards," she repeated and kissed me again. "I love the sound of 'our standards.' I have really missed us doing things together."

I looked at my beautiful wife and just smiled because, to be honest, I had missed that as well.

"So notepads to start making lists," I said.

"And then we give her a first bath," Fran said.

"Her?" I asked.

"Absolutely," Fran said, smiling. "She'll tell us her name as we go. Any idea how long this project might take?"

"If we get a lot of different people working on different parts," I said, "I was kind of hoping we could have it done in about nine months. No promises, of course, since both of us are new at this, but if we can do that, we can take a ride in it on the anniversary of your parent's death."

She stopped, looked at me, then burst into tears and hugged me like I hadn't been hugged since the first years of our marriage.

In time, and with a lot of money, they just might turn that pile of junk in the garage to a shining classic car.

Who knew that Ramblers, one of the most dull family cars to ever travel the highways could be so important to someone. Especially someone like Fran. But that pile of junk had now come to symbolize our marriage.

It was going to take time and a lot of work, but maybe, just maybe, we could get it running again. Both the car and the marriage.

And I liked that idea a lot.

DEAN WESLEY SMITH

She Collected
Very Special Stones
For Very Special Memories

THE STONE
SLEPT HERE

THE STONE SLEPT HERE

Jennifer Bends collects stones. Special stones.

She puts her stones on a shelf, both of them. No one asks about them because the stones are plain, heavy, pointless.

But the stones contain memories for Jennifer.

Nothing on Bryant Street is ever pointless.

———

The stone didn't look like much at first glance. Just a round rock, worn smooth through hundreds and hundreds of years of the blue waters of the Boise River moving over it.

Gray in color, even when wet and under bright sunlight, which was how Jennifer Bends found the stone when she was thirteen. She hadn't changed it at all. She liked it gray and round and simple.

She had been down on the riverbank under the Eagle Street Bridge with her mother and sister on a hot July day. The river water was cool, not cold, and not very deep. No real current existed where they waded since most of the river water went along the other tree-lined side.

The air of the late afternoon was hot, with little wind, but the river made everything smell fresh. And she was covered in suntan lotion, which she loved the smell of as well.

Where she found the rock was in a large pool of water that only came up to her knees. She had enjoyed just sitting in the pool, letting the cool water take away any thought of problems or boys in school or homework or how her mom barely afforded to buy them clothes and books.

When her hand touched the stone and she picked it up, she knew it was perfect. It was about the size of a sandwich. She fell in love with the stone at once. Smooth and warm and wonderful in her hand, she couldn't put it down.

And the stone was heavy enough to be important.

It always would remind her of that wonderful hot July afternoon on the river with her mother and older sister.

That day had been the best day they had had since her father had vanished earlier in the spring. Jennifer knew where he was, but she never told anyone, because her father had hurt her mother.

Now it was just Jennifer and her sister and her mom and that day along the riverbank proved they could be happy without their father.

Maybe a lot happier.

Jennifer took the stone home with her, even though her mother shook her head when she saw it.

Jennifer put it on her window ledge in her bedroom next to a similar large, gray stone. They could have almost been twins.

The two stones were always there, through junior high, then high school.

The two stones slept side-by-side when she came home from college and when she met Frank, the man she thought was the love of her life.

Jennifer had turned into an attractive woman, with short brown hair and large brown eyes. Men liked her, and she liked them, but staying with one just hadn't happened until Frank, the tall, strong, black-haired man with an easy smile and rough hands.

She got a job teaching grade school out of college and Frank worked at a tire store.

She moved the two stones to their new small starter home, just letting them rest on a shelf, occasionally holding up some books.

But then Frank turned out to be anything but a love of her life.

More like a monster of the night.

One month into their April marriage, she found out he was sleeping with another woman, an old girlfriend. And she asked him about it and he called her names she should not have been called.

No self-respecting woman should ever be called, actually.

And for a moment he looked like he might hit her as she stood her ground, facing him.

Then he had stormed out to go drinking and when he finally came home, almost too drunk to walk, she took the stone she had found in the river that wonderful day with her mom and sister and hit him over the back of the head with it when he wasn't looking.

He went down hard.

Out like a light.

No blood, thankfully.

She put a black plastic bag over his head, tied it off tight around his neck, then put another one over his head and tied it as well. Then she hit him in the head as hard as she could a few dozen more times with the stone.

The stone felt solid in her hands. After a time, Frank's head did not feel solid under the stone.

That was exactly as she had done with her daddy when he came home drunk that night after hitting her mother. She wanted to make sure he would never wake up.

Her daddy never woke up.

Frank would never wake up.

Then Jennifer washed her stone off carefully, with bleach, and put it back on the shelf next to the other stone.

Her father's stone.

With the help of a wheelbarrow that Frank had not understood why she wanted to buy, she got him out of the house and into his car, the black bag still securely wrapped around his head to make sure no blood got anywhere.

His car was a blue Mercedes that she had discovered after they were married that he couldn't afford on his salary at the tire store.

Driving very carefully, with him slouched in the passenger seat with a baseball cap over the bag on his head, she took him to the woods behind her mother's house and buried him next to her father.

It was the same spot she could see from her childhood window.

Her mother still lived there in that house.

The woods there were tall pine, with thick underbrush. A seldom-used dirt road went through the edge of the large stand of trees. The area had been declared wetlands and no one could build on it at all. Besides, Jennifer knew the neighbors around the wetlands liked the large area of trees and water and the small stream that flowed through the trees. It gave their neighborhood class.

Jennifer then put on a pair of Frank's coveralls he used at work. They were black with a few patches on them, so they would help her stay hidden in the dark. And she had brought old tennis shoes and an extra pair of socks to change into when finished.

It took Jennifer four hours of digging in the soft spring soil, but she got the job done and then covered up any sign that she had been there as best she could.

In a month or so, the underbrush would cover it all.

No one had found her daddy there. No one would find her husband either.

Then she took his car to a spot near their small starter home and parked it on the bank of the Boise River, pointing down into the fast river, roaring with the spring runoff. She smudged up the steering wheel and key to make sure both her prints and his prints were on the car.

She changed out of her dirt-covered shoes and walked on the rocks down to the river and tossed them in.

She took off his coveralls and tossed them on the front seat, opened both windows full, and made sure no one was around at all, anywhere.

Then she put the car in gear and let it go down the hill and into the fast water.

It tipped over at once and was swept away downriver, sinking out of sight in the dark water.

Staying in the shadows and hiding any time a car even came close, she walked the few blocks home. Then she made sure that there was no blood or anything showing on the hardwood floor where she had hit him.

No sign.

Nothing.

Then she kissed both rocks goodnight and went to bed.

The next day at school, she was called out of class with the bad news that they had found his car in the river. The two detectives asked her if he had come home last night.

She did her best to act like the worried wife, saying that he was angry when he left, despondent, went to drink. And had never come home.

The detectives told her that he had been drinking until about one in the morning and at which bar. She knew it was the one his old girlfriend worked at.

They told her there were tire tracks that matched his car going into the river near their home.

She told them that he loved that car, that they had only been married a month, and made them promise to do everything they could to find him.

Of course, a year later, no one had found him.

After two years, she filed for divorce and got it.

About that point, she started dating again.

It was during a wonderful trip with her new boyfriend to the Oregon Coast that she found the third rock.

Her boyfriend named Craig knew about how Frank had vanished, leaving her a month after they had married. He treated her with respect and a gentle touch.

And he didn't drink.

He was the one, actually, that found the stone for her.

He came up to where she sat on the beach in a lounge chair, staring at the beautiful ocean. He was holding a stone about the same size as the other two she had in her collection.

The new stone was smooth like her other two, worn down through time in the water. It also was plain and simple and felt important when she held it in her hand.

"It's perfect," she had said, smiling up at him. "Just perfect."

"I hoped you would like it," he said.

"I like it more than you can imagine," she said, kissing him.

And when they got back to Boise, she put the rock on her fireplace mantle with her other two rocks.

They all slept together there, looking peaceful.

Six months later, she and Craig were married.

So far things were going smoothly.

So far.

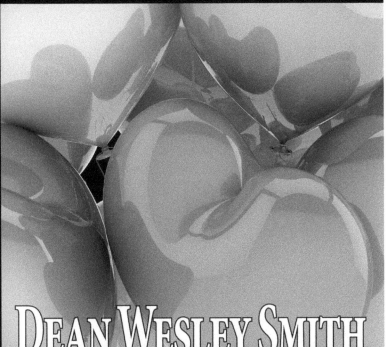

Smith's
STORIES

DEAN WESLEY SMITH
IT'S MY PARTY
A Bryant Street Story

BRYANT STREET

IT'S MY PARTY

A woman decides to throw a surprise birthday party for her husband. She decorates, gets out the snacks and beer, and is ready for the party.

Only this party takes place on Bryant Street.

No party on Bryant Street works as intended. Or maybe it does.

———

Julie Reinhart stepped back from the decorated living room of her three-bedroom home on Bryant Street and studied what she had just completed. Along the blinds over the front window looking out at the sunny day and the green lawns beyond, she had hung streamers of bright blue and orange and green. And numbers of balloons mostly red and orange and yellow hung from the blinds.

On the mantel of the stone fireplace, she had a huge sign that said "Happy Birthday" in hand-drawn and colorful letters. And she had balloons everywhere of all colors, tied with colorful ribbons and hanging from the bookshelves on both sides of the couch.

It had taken her all morning to blow up all those balloons, but it had been worth it, since they really gave the room a festive feel.

She had "Happy Birthday" colored napkins scattered on the coffee tables and end tables giving the entire room the final blast of celebration colors.

"Perfect," she said to herself and then turned back to the similarly decorated dining room. She had hung a big hand-lettered sign on the sliding door out to the backyard. The sign read, "Happy 30th!!!"

She had outdone herself this year, she knew it without a doubt. But her wonderful husband, Frank, deserved the best and he was going to love this, with all his friends showing up to help him celebrate. A guy didn't turn thirty that often, after all.

She checked the fridge to make sure there were enough beer and other beverages, and enough extra ice to last. There was.

And the cupboards were stuffed with chips and pretzels and other snacks, including cans of peanuts. She didn't need to get those out until people started showing up.

She headed down the hallway to their master bedroom where she changed into her party dress and made sure her long brown hair was combed and tied back like Frank liked it.

Then she glanced at her watch. Ten minutes until five. The guests should start arriving at any point now and Frank would be here at five thirty, just as he did every night.

She went back out into the kitchen, looked around at everything once more and then smiled. She had done well.

The house looked like a party.

She sat down at the kitchen table, feeling tired. Surprisingly tired. And empty.

She put her head down on her arm and closed her eyes. Maybe she could just rest until the first guest knocked.

Two hours later she awoke with a start. She had been drooling slightly on her arm and it was asleep and tingling.

She glanced around at all the decorations, then glanced at her watch. Seven in the evening and it was nearing dusk outside.

She nodded to herself and turned on the lights in the dining room and a couple of the lamps in the living room. Then with the end of a safety pin, she popped all the balloons along the front window, took off the colorful decorations and pulled the blinds closed.

In thirty minutes she had all the decorations down and in garbage bags and her living room and dining room back to their normal pristine condition.

She stored the two signs in the garage next to her new Lexus. She would put them in the attic above the garage tomorrow.

She put the bags of decorations in the garbage. Then she went back inside and moved the bags of chips and beer into the pantry. Then she changed out of her party dress into her kick-around-the-house sweatpants and light sweatshirt, and made herself a tuna salad to go along with a glass of red wine.

She sat at the dining table eating slowly and savoring the wine.

Then at five minutes until eight, she raised the glass into the air and said simply, "It would have been a great party, Frank. Always love you."

Then as she was cleaning up her dishes from dinner, the door from the garage opened and the love of her life, Cynthia Davis, came in.

Cynthia was dressed in her office clothes, her long blond hair pulled back, a black briefcase that matched her black jacket and slacks was in her hand.

Cynthia came up behind Julie at the sink and hugged her from behind. Then as Cynthia moved to put her brief- case on the dining room table she asked, "How was the party?"

"Just like every year," Julie said as she finished up putting her dishes in the dishwasher. "It would have been a great party."

"You think it is still helping?" Cynthia asked, leaning against the table and looking at Julie with a worried expression.

"I honestly don't know if it's helping like it did twenty

years ago," Julie said. "But it's not hurting either. And gives me a few hours to remember Frank each year on his birthday. I honestly don't think much about him the rest of the year anymore. Kind of sad, actually."

Cynthia nodded. "I just worry that it keeps that horrible night fresh as well."

Julie shook her head. "I don't think about what actually happened that night. I don't even dream about getting that call anymore from the police and seeing the pictures of the accident. That part is all tucked away in the past. Staging the party just helps me remember how much I cared about him."

"And that is valuable," Cynthia said. "And I miss him as well."

"How did your remembrance go?" Julie asked.

"I rented the same room we used that afternoon, like always," Cynthia said. "After twenty years it is getting a little run down."

"I bet," Julie said.

"I ordered two glasses of champagne just as Frank and I did that afternoon, and just took my clothes off and stretched out on the bed to remember him. I fell asleep just as I do every year, now."

"Yeah, I fell asleep at the table again," Julie said. "Does it still help you?"

"More of what you said. It helps me remember him once a year. Like you, I don't think about him otherwise. And yes, that is sad."

"Too bad he didn't make it to the party," Cynthia said. "It would have been so much fun to see his face after everyone left and you and I were in the bedroom together, naked."

Julie laughed. "Yeah, that would have been a birthday to remember. He just had no idea how good that birthday party was going to be."

"So do we still do this every year to mourn him or celebrate him bringing us together without even knowing he was doing that?"

Julie just smiled and went over to Cynthia and hugged her. "I think it's a little mourning of a man we both loved, but lately it has become a celebration of you and me in my mind."

"Mine too," Cynthia said. "So you think the guests would all be gone by now from the party?"

"I do," Julie said, smiling.

"So lets go get naked together in that big bed and show Frank what he missed by hitting that truck on his way from me to you."

"Think he can see us?" Julie asked, laughing as they headed down the hall.

"Oh, I really hope so," Cynthia said, also laughing.

"If he can see us, it will serve him right," Julie said, "for him having an affair with the love of my life."

"Yeah, that will teach him," Cynthia said. "At least for his next life."

"You think?" Julie asked.

Cynthia pretended to consider the question, then laughed and shook her head. "Frank? Not a chance."

"So true," Julie said as she watched Cynthia get undressed. "But that night you got to admit, it would have been a hell of a party."

"And it will be tonight," Cynthia said, "if you ever get out of those clothes."

DEAN WESLEY SMITH

WINGS OUT
A Bryant Street Story

WINGS OUT

Rolanda Campbell finds herself living a life she never could have imagined.

A prison life on a simple suburban street called Bryant Street.

She knew she bore the responsibility for the horrid life.

So finally she took the responsibility for leaving as well. And never once looked back at Bryant Street.

————

This would be the last time.

Rolanda Campbell stretched and stood from her recliner, looking around the modern living room, dark because of the blinds being pulled against the sun.

A long, uncomfortable couch he had picked out to match an even more uncomfortable love seat filled one wall in front of the window, its off-yellow color looking like dried puke in the wrong light.

The fake-stone fireplace had never been used, of course. Too dirty.

Her tan recliner facing the large screen television mounted over the fireplace matched his, and with two pillows she had managed to make it comfortable for her thin, five-five frame.

Out of habit she fluffed the two pillows and put them back exactly where they belonged on the couch.

Then, just for the hell of it, she tossed the pillows into the middle of the living room floor. That would drive the bastard nuts.

This morning would be the last time she would ever watch those morning shows and deal with the pressure of trying to be perfect for a man who didn't know perfect, but believed he did.

Every morning now for three years, since their honeymoon, Rolanda had gotten out of bed ahead of her husband, showered, dressed as if she was going to a business meeting in expensive pantsuits, put on makeup as he expected her to do, and made him breakfast.

The exact same breakfast. Same two eggs over easy, same white toast with strawberry jam, same slice of ham. Heaven help her if she overcooked his eggs.

She would have been so much more comfortable in jeans and tennis shoes and a cotton blouse, but he wanted her to look her best for him when he left for work. She had caved in to that demand, just as he had worn her down and forced her into this life in the first place.

Then she ate lightly with him at the breakfast table because he didn't want her to get fat.

Then as she did the dishes, he read his morning journals on his iPad without saying a word, then put it in his brief-case, kissed her on the cheek, thanked her for breakfast, and left for work.

All very civil and cold.

Dead cold.

Rolanda's job was to keep the house spotless and have dinner ready for him when he got home. Which she had done for three long, stupid years.

Then they watched a prescribed amount of television together, always what he wanted to watch, then went to bed at the exact same time every night.

Sex had long become a thing of the past for them.

What they were living was his sick image of a perfect marriage.

Perfect in his mind, not in hers.

She had a master's in interior design and had married him right out of school, thinking they would be a perfect match. Instead she had made herself in three short years into a prisoner to a man she now detested.

One year ago, she had finally hit her limit and tried to talk with him about what she wasn't happy about. At that point she still thought the marriage might be saved.

She really was that stupid.

It was a first marriage and she had no other family. She had no way of knowing otherwise.

He would have none of her problems. They were married, she was his wife, she would not leave him, she would do as he asked.

End of discussion.

Things went right back to the way they had been as if nothing had happened.

To her own disgust at herself, she had backed down.

And shut up.

It wasn't as if he hit her. He never had.

She doubted he ever would.

But she had become deathly afraid of him anyway. And she had no idea why.

She desperately needed to understand why in the very near future. But for now, she had things to do today, not normal things, very different things.

It was time she took her life back.

Six months ago she had saved enough from the grocery money he allowed her to hire a private detective to see what the bastard husband did every day. It took her a few thousand, but she finally discovered bastard husband went to work as an accountant as he said he did, but was sleeping with a waitress from a restaurant three lunches a day.

If she confronted him with the fact, he would either deny it or say it was his right as a man to do just that. After all, didn't he provide the perfect home for her and pay all the bills?

So Rolanda hadn't said a word, just kept doing her "job" as he expected.

But it was with that discovery she had decided to finally take back her pride and finish this entire thing.

She clicked off the morning shows and acting as calm as the bastard always did, she moved to the house computer in an alcove off the dining room. She had hired help from a local computer store to come and undo all the locks and safety features the bastard husband had put on the home computer to keep her contained.

Using the files the detective had given her, and accounts she had opened under her maiden name in three banks, she moved all of their money to her accounts.

It was a lot more money than she had expected because until that moment she had never dared check the accounts. But honestly she didn't care. She left him none of it.

Not one penny.

She called the attorney she had hired a few months before and said to serve the divorce papers on the bastard.

The woman attorney, named Steph, said, "With pleasure."

The attorney had pictures of Rolanda's bastard husband with the waitress, so no divorce would be contested. Not even with an ego like the bastard husband had. He didn't dare show that side of himself in public. That would shatter the illusion of perfection he worked too hard to maintain.

And that Rolanda had gone along with.

Steph had asked Rolanda if she wanted the house, since

she could get it in the divorce, but all that had done was make her shudder. She just wanted out.

With that all done, she then called her husband's boss, a man by the name of Stratton.

She knew her husband would be in the hotel room with the waitress at that point.

She asked if he was alone and they could talk.

Stratton said he was.

She then told him that she was divorcing her husband for infidelity, but today when she got access to their accounts, she realized he had a lot more money than should be there and there was evidence her husband had been moving some money into other accounts she couldn't access.

"Are you being vindictive?" Stratton asked, his voice cold.

"No," she said, lying through her teeth. "I could be, but I am far past that, to be honest. I am leaving my husband because he has been screwing a waitress. I am just trying to do you a service is all and tell you what I found today when I got my money from his accounts. You might want to investigate quietly. The private detective I hired thinks he saw some pretty fishy things as well. But that is up to you. It is your business. I honestly don't care."

With that she hung up, smiling.

Her husband's perfect life was just going to be messed up something awful today.

She knew, without a doubt or excuse, that she had been at fault for letting him do this to her. She flat knew that. She had only wanted her marriage to work and at first she had been happy to go along.

Not anymore.

Once she got settled in her new life and found a job in her profession, the first thing she would do would be to find a counselor and figure out why she had allowed herself to get into this situation.

And stay in it for so long.

She had a hunch it was because of the fear of suddenly being alone in the large world and her perfect husband gave her the foundation she had needed for a short time.

But she had allowed it to go on for three years.

She knew she never would again.

She moved into their bedroom, the last time she would ever be in that room, and took out the two packed suitcases from the back of the closet, then changed into jeans, tennis shoes, and a cotton blouse. She left all the expensive pantsuits he had wanted her to wear hanging in the closet.

His dozen suits, all matching dark blue, hung in rows on his side of the closet, everything in its perfect place, his dark shoes lined up below the suits.

She went to the bathroom and got a small bottle of acid from under the sink where she had hidden it. It was for burning off corns, but it put really nice holes in fabric.

She carefully put one drop of acid on each suit coat, right behind the shoulder where it would be clear to anyone and impossible to fix, one drop of acid on the toe of each shoe, and one drop of acid on the crotch of each of his slacks.

Then she sprinkled the rest of the acid on his perfectly folded underwear in his drawer. She had folded them all.

His perfect look was soon going to have some holes in it.

That made her laugh for the first time in longer than she could remember.

The sound seemed very strange in that bedroom.

She glanced at the clock.

Mr. Perfect Husband would now be halfway done with his mistress. The papers would be served to him when they came walking out in about fifteen minutes. Even in an affair, the bastard was punctual and predictable and boring.

But right now, Rolanda needed to vanish.

She needed to move on with her life, but just for fun, she had one more little annoyance to toss at Mr. Perfect.

One more stab into whatever tiny little heart the man had. If she could get through his ego to even reach his heart.

She left her driver's license with her married name on the dresser along with the one credit card he allowed her for groceries and to buy clothes. She already had a new credit card and a new driver's license under her maiden name.

She put her phone beside the license. She already had a new phone as well.

And under that she pulled out of her second drawer a picture of Mr. Perfect and the waitress. Both were naked. The shot had been taken with a long-range camera by the detective. The lawyer had a copy of that photo and some other choice ones as well.

Under the picture Rolanda had a note that said, "If you

want your wife to be perfect, you must also be perfect. Just a suggestion for your next wife."

Then she pulled out her new phone and called for a ride from the private detective she had hired. He was standing by in a café four blocks away just in case she ran into trouble today.

The detective was a great guy. Handsome, clearly talented, and he liked her. Given a little time, who knew where that would lead.

But first she needed the time to be alone, to be in her own place, to live the way she wanted to live.

She needed to fly on her own for a while.

And not be perfect.

With two suitcases in hand, she walked to the front door and looked back at the home she had cleaned continuously for three straight years.

She glanced out the window. Her detective friend wasn't here yet, so maybe just one or two more little things to stab at Mr. Perfect just a little more.

She went to the closet and took out the vacuum cleaner and plugged it in, then with the cord spread along the ground and around a couple chairs, she left the vacuum in the hallway right in front of the front door.

She turned on the television, fairly loud, and tossed the remotes into the garbage can under the sink, under the morning's waste where he would never look for them.

She left the dishwasher door standing open.

And then she opened all the blinds in the living room,

letting in the sunshine, something he never allowed for fear it would fade the furniture.

There was now light where there had been darkness.

As she looked out the window, the private detective pulled up.

She grabbed her two suitcases and, skipping like a college girl, headed down the front sidewalk, leaving the front door wide open.

She never looked back at the prison she had made for herself.

She had finally escaped.

She was now free. Free to fly.

And she planned on doing a lot of flying.

Smith's
STORIES

Dean Wesley Smith

Stranger in the Shadows
A Bryant Street Story

STRANGER IN THE SHADOWS

David Maguire, in his beautiful home on Bryant Street, suddenly starts seeing ghosts.

But not just any ghosts, but future residents of his own home.

That would be enough by itself to bother a guy. But the reason behind the ghosts turns out far, far worse.

———

ONE

David Maguire woke with a start. There were other people in the bedroom.

He could sense it.

Alicia was still asleep beside him in their big king bed, her face turned toward the wall away from him.

This was the third time this week he had come awake

with a sense of someone in the room. Tonight it was more intense than ever.

He eased over the edge of the bed and put on his bathrobe from where he had left it draped over his night-stand. He made himself take shallow breaths to calm his racing heart and then moved back from the bed slightly so that he was in the shadows cast from the faint nightlight in the master bathroom.

His robe was dark, his hair dark. So chances are no one could see him.

As he watched, he felt the hairs on his arms rise and the air turn suddenly cold.

Then there was another bed in the room, a shadow bed, queen-sized with a pattern comforter on it. It was turned to be against the bathroom wall, and there was a small couch and chair in front of the window that looked out over the backyard.

A young couple, a man in his thirties and a woman about the same age came out of the bathroom, smiling and talking. They were also shadow figures. David could see right through them like they were ghosts.

He didn't think they were ghosts, but he did know they scared him more than he had ever been scared before.

The couple looked as if they had just come back from a party. The man had on a suit jacket and jeans and the woman had on a nice summer dress with low heels.

David couldn't hear what they were saying, and after a moment they faded and were gone along with the bed and their furniture.

He stood there for the longest time, working to catch his breath. He knew these people couldn't have lived here in the past. He and Alicia had built this house here in this wonderful subdivision. They called the house their dream home until the dream of their marriage had turned sour with the arrival of their twins.

Nothing had been the same after that. He remembered when he and Alicia used to go out and come back home just as that young couple had done, laughing and talking and maybe making love.

Those years were long in the past now. The twins were six and the dreams and the marriage were dead. They were basically just on cruise control because of the boys, going through the motions, pretending to be happy.

That pretending and being trapped in this house had worn on him more and more over the last few years. Yet he had no way out.

He sat up for a couple hours until it felt safe to go back to bed, where his alarm woke him a few short hours later so that he could start another mundane, boring, lifeless day.

TWO

Alicia was already up and in the kitchen by the time David got out of the shower and finished dressing for work. His job was accounting and he had loved it at one time in his life. Now it was just work.

Now that the twins were in school, Alicia had gone back to work at the University. She said she liked her job, but they had never really talked much about it. They were using all the money she made to save for the twins' college.

As he stood looking in the mirror, another ghost bed appeared, this one different and overlapping their bed. The furniture in the room also looked different.

This time two men came out of the bathroom together, both dressed as if going to work in high-tech. Both were about David's height and they clearly were a couple.

The air around David seemed to crackle and get colder once again. David just stood completely still, even though he was sure they couldn't see him.

They were talking and David could again not tell what they were saying.

After a few moments that seemed to stretch, they vanished and then their furniture did as well.

So two couples living in the same room, the same house, more than likely.

If it hadn't been so real, David would have assumed he was dreaming. But this didn't feel like a dream.

Not in the slightest.

That night, even though he was exhausted, he couldn't sleep. He just lay there staring at the ceiling.

After about forty minutes, the air snapped cold once again.

This time David sat up, but just stayed in bed as another group of bedroom furniture appeared and a very different couple came walking out of the bathroom. This was an older couple, well into their sixties. He was bald and she had short, silver hair.

They were both dressed in what looked like silk pajamas.

Their bed was turned against the bathroom wall and as they climbed into bed, they both stopped suddenly and looked around.

Then the woman said softly to the husband, "Do you see the ghost?"

The husband nodded and whispered. "Sitting in his bed staring at us."

"I'm not a ghost," David said. "You are the ghosts."

With that both jerked and eased closer to each other.

"What is your name, son," the man asked after a moment.

David looked at them, then said, "David Maguire and this is my house. Who are you?"

The woman gasped and covered her mouth. The man just kept staring as he sat there on the bed.

"Rose and Stan Fields," the man said. "And you are the ghost I'm afraid, son. Twenty years ago you killed your wife and kids and then yourself, right out there in the garage."

"I would never do that," David said, shocked at the very idea.

"If you would never do that," the old man said, "why are you haunting us?"

"You're haunting me," David said. "You and the others."

Stan laughed. Let me guess, a young, active-looking couple and two gay men. Right? I saw pictures of them.

They all loved this place, never said anything about a ghost."

David nodded, trying to keep his mind under control.

"They owned the house after you and before we bought it," the old man said. "We knew the home's history. We're not the type who believed in ghosts. Guess we were wrong about that, huh, Rose."

Rose only nodded, clearly too afraid to speak.

"I'm not a ghost," David said, barely containing the panic he was feeling. "Alicia, my wife is right here beside me in bed."

Stan looked at Rose, then back at David. "If what you say is right, then don't buy that shotgun. Let your twins grow up and you and your wife fix your problems and live to be old farts like us."

With that, the older couple and their bed and furniture were gone.

Stan climbed out of bed, put on his bathrobe, and left the room. He was shaking so badly he barely made it to the kitchen.

Two hours later, Alica found him sitting at their kitchen table just staring at the wall.

"You all right?" she asked as she went to get a glass of water.

"No," he said. "I'm not all right and neither are we."

She stopped and turned to face him. Her eyes were cold, as they had often been lately.

"Are you willing to go get some couples counseling

with me?" he asked her, staring into her eyes. "See if we can get back to being happy again?"

She stood there, clearly shocked. Then she slowly nodded. "Yes."

In her eyes, behind the cold, protected dullness, he could see a glimmer of the Alicia he had fallen in love with.

"Any chance we can get a sitter for the twins tomorrow, drop them with your mom or something after school, you call in for a personal day, I'll call in for the same, and we'll just spend the day together? Just the two of us. Could you do that? Would you want to do that?"

She stared at him, then nodded. "Is it a special day?"

"It's June 19th," he said. "And it will be a special day if we make it one."

She nodded to that.

"No plans," he said. "I just want to spend the day with the woman I love. And maybe we can talk about how we are going to change where we find ourselves at the moment."

She had tears in her eyes as she stepped toward him. He stood and they hugged, really hugged, for the first time in as long as he could remember.

And it felt wonderful.

THREE

David was working on the shrubs along the front of his home.

The sun was warm but not hot, one of those perfect

early summer days when the smell of freshly mowed grass seemed to fill the air.

Every year in the early summer he had to cut the shrubs and trim them. He had been doing that now for the thirty years they had owned the home.

He was now doing freelance accounting from one of the twins' old bedrooms and Alicia had gotten her teaching certificate and was enjoying teaching. The twins had both graduated college and gotten married and he was the proud grandfather of three now.

Talking with Stan and Rose Fields had haunted him almost every day. It had taken most of a year of counseling for David and Alicia to get back on track with their marriage. It hadn't just been him who was unhappy, but Alicia had thought about leaving him numbers of times.

A year after the short talk with Stan and Rose, David tracked them down in real life. They were a happy forty-something couple with grandkids and two kids in college. David hadn't bothered them because he was certain they wouldn't understand.

He wasn't sure he completely understood.

All he knew was that what they had told him he would do to Alice and his kids made him sick to his stomach. The idea of not seeing his kids grow up and his grandkids was just too much. He could not even imagine it.

So he had made sure that when he and Alicia had a problem, they worked on it at once.

And since he and Alicia started changing things, Stan

and Rose or anyone else for that matter were never moving into his home, so there had been no more ghost sightings.

He had never told Alicia about the visions or dreams or whatever he had.

He and Alicia had changed the future and got the feeling of this being their dream home back again. Instead of the house being a trap for David, it had become a place he always wanted to be.

But that attitude switch had taken most of a year to make. He was very glad that he and Alicia did the work to make it happen.

Now, if he could just get the bushes cut back before Alicia got home. They celebrated every year on June 19th, the anniversary of him asking her if they wanted to get counseling and the wonderful, learning day that had followed.

And the learning year that had followed as well.

They called June 19th their rebirth day.

"Nice place," a voice behind him said.

David turned around to see Stan and Rose Fields smiling at him from the sidewalk.

They looked exactly as he remembered them that night in the bedroom.

It took him a moment to get past his shock.

They couldn't be ghosts, could they? But it was on the anniversary of the last time he saw them.

Finally, he said, "Thanks."

"We just moved into the Steven's place," Stan said. "Four doors up the street."

"So I guess we are neighbors," Rose said, her smiling beaming.

With that David smiled, letting the relief flood through him. "Well welcome to the neighborhood. It's a great place to live."

"How long you lived here?" Stan asked.

"Thirty years," David said. And he could feel the pride in his voice with that.

Stan whistled. "Think we can make it that long?" he asked Rose with a smile.

She laughed and gave him a friendly push along the sidewalk. "If we keep exercising, we just might get that lucky."

And with a wave they were off, walking together, enjoying the wonderful, sunny day.

David watched them move away.

Lucky.

He supposed he had been lucky, to haunt them and have them tell him the truth.

Now, twenty-one years ago to the day they had returned. This really was a very strange neighborhood.

He looked up the tree-lined street, very thankful that he lived here. It was a beautiful and strange place.

Then whistling, he went back to trimming the shrubs.

Smith's
STORIES

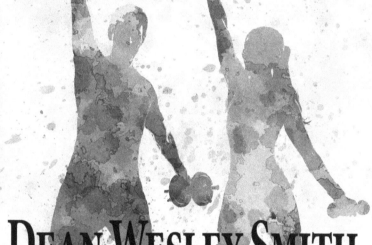

DEAN WESLEY SMITH
USA Today Bestselling Writer

SOMETHING IN MY DARLING
A Bryant Street Story

SOMETHING IN MY DARLING

Canning Boone starts noticing something changed with his wife Jenny when they moved onto Bryant Street. Of all things she seemed happy. And talked about losing weight.

Shocked and horrified described Canning's reaction. And she lost the weight. Canning knew he must do something. But what?

———

Canning Boone started to suspect something was wrong with Jenny a few days after they moved into their wonderful, three bedroom ranch home on Bryant Street.

She started smiling more.

Now Jenny, with her long brown hair, her round green eyes, and her solid, some would say obese body, had always laughed and smiled at times. Usually when eating.

But after they got settled in their new home, with their

new kitchen and wonderful large recliners in front of the massive television screen, she started smiling more and talking about all sorts of wild stuff.

She mentioned losing weight.

That was the first time in six years of marriage she had used the term "losing weight." He would have been less surprised if she had said she was watching internet porn.

When she said that, he froze in his recliner, a spoonful of mashed potatoes halfway to his mouth from his dinner tray.

She went on not realizing he was shocked to his core and almost unable to take another bite. She said she loved the house so much that she wanted to get fit and enjoy it more, work in the yard on the flowers, maybe even plant a garden.

Canning managed to get back to eating, listening to her go on about such horrific ideas.

Now Canning hadn't married Jenny to have her suddenly get happy and thin and active. He had married her because he loved her pessimism, her often sharp and nasty way of looking at the world, and her ability to eat just about anything.

She could match him bite-for-bite.

He had never met a woman who could. That was why he fell in love with her, actually.

And he really loved her complete lack of any desire to do the things he hated, like sports or even walking too far.

The very idea of working in a garden just made him shudder. He paid thin people to do that.

So at first, for months, Canning ignored Jenny, nodding

when he needed to, making no comments, hoping they would just settle into their normal routine. But then one morning she announced she had joined a gym and would be going there in the afternoon on her break from her job at Walmart.

He said nothing and she just smiled as she packed some "workout" clothes she had bought a few days before, showing him each bit of the outfit.

He managed to not shudder at the term "workout" and got off to his government job with a kiss from Jenny and one of her now frequent smiles.

But the day was ruined and not even four times through a buffet at lunch made him feel better.

What in the world had happened?

The only thing he could figure was that it was their new home.

Or the subdivision. Maybe the Bryant Street Subdivision had cursed her.

He laughed at that thought and didn't even ask how her "workout" went.

But then he noticed that even though their meals together were normal in time and location in front of the television, she started eating less, not finishing platefuls of food as their parents had taught them.

And one night when they were out at their favorite Chinese restaurant, she even asked for a doggy bag to take some food home.

Shocked didn't begin to describe how he was feeling.

Socked and sad.

DEAN WESLEY SMITH

And afraid for Jenny's well-being. Since they had moved to Bryant Street, she seemed to be changing her personality. And there didn't seem to be a damn thing he could say about it.

So like any husband in his situation would do, he ate and said nothing. But he did a great deal of nodding.

As the next months went by, she showed him new cloths she had bought and by the end of six months it was clear she was really sick because she had lost so much weight. She would cook for him and then cook something different for herself. Usually something green.

They would eat in front of the television, but she would have one bite to his ten.

That was just wrong.

Even worse, the more weight she lost, the more energy she had. And the more energy she had, the more she talked about losing weight.

A horrid fifth circle of hell as far as he was concerned.

He had no doubt she was no longer the woman he had married. She didn't even look like the same woman.

Finally he could take it no longer.

"We need to move," he said.

"No," she said, not even turning from the sink where she was washing off some sort of cabbage.

If he hadn't already been sitting solidly on one of their heavy, wooden kitchen chairs, he might have fallen to the ground. And in Jenny's weakened condition and lighter weight, she never would have been able to help him up.

"No?" he asked.

78

"No," she said. "I like it here, this is my dream home, and I am staying."

"You can't afford to stay if I want to go," he said, deciding to be male macho, something he never had been and didn't play well.

She turned to him with one of those horrid new smiles on her face. "I forgot to tell you, but I am now a manager at the store, and I can afford this place better than you can."

"But this isn't who you are," he said. "I loved you for who you were, not this new person."

"I know," she said, still smiling. "You loved me because I had rolls of fat, because I could eat with you and as much as you, because I was as unhappy as you are every day. That was how we bonded."

"And what is wrong with that?"

Damn he wished he hadn't asked that question, but there it was, right out there in the kitchen.

"I don't want to be that person anymore," she said simply, going back to washing off the vegetables in the sink. "I want to have energy, look at the world in a positive way, and be healthy."

"So what happened?" he asked, almost afraid of the answer.

She motioned around at the house. "I found the house of my dreams, the neighborhood I love, and a man I love with you. I decided I wanted to enjoy it, keep the house up, work on the yard and what needs to be done to this wonderful home, not just wallow inside it."

He saw nothing at all wrong with wallowing, but he

said nothing. It was as he had feared, the house, the street had done this to her.

And he was going to lose her if he wasn't careful, if he already hadn't lost her.

That thought just scared him to death.

"So what do you want me to do?"

She beamed, a smile larger than he had ever seen before, and he had to admit, it made her more beautiful.

She wiped off her hands and opened a drawer and pulled out a folder and slid it to him. "I want you to make an appointment with this counselor and just talk with him."

"About what?" Canning asked, looking at the folder like it might just turn into a snake and bite him. He had a hunch what was in that folder was worse than any snake.

"About anything," she said. "I started going to her and talking with her soon after we moved in here because I wanted to understand why I couldn't enjoy this wonderful house."

"Will she help me understand what is happening with you?" he asked.

She smiled and nodded. "If that is important to you, yes."

"It is all that matters," he said.

With that she came over to him and kissed him. She was smiling, but there were tears in her eyes.

"Thank you," she said.

There just wasn't anything more he could say to that.

So he opened the folder and the snake bit him.

It took exactly three years to the day before he finished

his first marathon run. He had started off at 410 pounds and ran the marathon at 165 pounds.

Scales in their bathroom were like gods they worshipped every day, sometimes twice a day.

Jenny had finished ahead of him in the marathon run, since this was her fifth. She was waiting and cheering for him at the finish line.

She gave him a huge smile and a long hug and then kiss.

He felt great about finishing, but what he really felt great about was that they could hit the buffet after the race and he could eat as much as he wanted. That was all he could think about for the last ten miles.

He and Jenny still bonded on the food.

And once again they could eat as much as they wanted. And when they wanted.

He still didn't much enjoy all the exercise to stay at the light weight. He doubted he ever would, but for Jenny's sake, he pretended to.

And they still lived on Bryant Street and Jenny took care of the yard and her garden. He didn't care.

All that mattered to him was that he could eat regular meals with Jenny.

Bite-for-bite. She matched him and he matched her.

And finally things were back to normal for them.

Smith's
STORIES

DEAN WESLEY SMITH
REMEMBERING
THE LAST LAUGH
A Bryant Street Short Story

BRYANT STREET

REMEMBERING THE LAST LAUGH

Bryant Street, where things just never seem right, never work right, never exist as expected. Most of the time.

I created Bryant Street a long time ago when Stephen King said writers should write about what scares them. Subdivisions terrify me at a deep level, so I created Bryant Street.

But sometimes the strange people who chose to live on Bryant Street end up happy. Even Bryant Street keeps surprising.

Sher Carr could not remember the last time she had laughed.

She could remember just about everything else. She never forgot a family birthday or her husband's schedule. She never forgot a meal and really enjoyed trying new recipes. And she never forgot garbage day or when it was time to clean a certain part of the house.

She never forgot a deadline with work or an appointment, either.

Yet for the life of her she couldn't remember the last time she had actually laughed.

She smiled a lot. People had told her she had a wonderful smile. But she never laughed and for the last couple days that was really bothering her, since reading an article online about how laughing was good for the health.

Sher considered herself a normal person. She stood five-four, was thin and in shape because she exercised three times a week in their home gym in the back bedroom. She had short blonde hair she kept styled and usually wore slacks, a nice matching blouse, and often a light sweater, dressing up for work even though she worked from an office in their third bedroom.

She was a project manager who worked for a number of corporations, almost entirely from home, since the companies she helped were spread all over the world. She found the work challenging and sometimes stressful. And it certainly paid well.

She and her husband Steve went out for dinner almost every Friday, usually at one of three of their favorite restaurants. They would talk about Steve's job at a major tech firm or her most recent client or work problem or even the plan for the next thing they wanted to do to fix up the house.

Every six months or so they talked about the family they

wanted to start, but they both felt young at thirty-one, so they had some time to wait.

They had pretty regular sex every Friday night after dinner and then worked together around the house on Saturday together. They had a wonderful three-bedroom home on a nice quiet street called Bryant Street.

They had nice, brown-toned cloth furniture, two new cars, both Fords, but not pets, since Steve was allergic to both cats and dogs.

They both really liked working on their home and taking pride in it. They had just remodeled their kitchen to state-of-the-art everything. That had made her smile almost every day since it was finished.

They also had good neighbors who kept their houses up perfectly as well. She loved their neighborhood. She felt safe in it.

She and Steve went to church on Sunday—Presbyterian —and had lunch afterward with family, sometimes her parents, sometimes his.

She enjoyed all aspects of her life and didn't feel unhappy.

But for the life of her she couldn't remember the last time she had laughed. That stupid article she had read a few days back had really gotten into her head. And now it was chewing up her morning.

She glanced at her calendar. She had no appointments this morning online, so she just sat at the kitchen table sipping on a cup of coffee and thinking.

She couldn't remember the last time Steve had laughed either.

Now granted, Steve had never much had a sense of humor. In fact she had fallen in love with him because of his drive and seriousness about the world issues. And his dream of a nice home and family matched hers completely.

As they had gotten older, their discussions about politics had faded back to more about jobs, money, and their house. She missed those old political discussions, even though they both were pretty much on the same side of things.

They took their commitment to each other very seriously as well. It didn't even occur to her to think about another man. She was happy with Steve, but he most certainly didn't make her laugh.

She wasn't sure how important that was, actually.

Laughter indicated joy in something. She was happy with just about everything, including their financial situation, her love, her family, but she didn't feel pure, laughter-inducing joy in anything.

And she had no idea why.

She had attained her dream in life to be happily married to a great man, have a great job that challenged her, have a nice home. She had it all, every piece of that young girl's dream except kids and both of them were just waiting for that, which was fine with her completely.

So what was wrong?

What was she missing?

Or was it something as simple as she never laughed?

Had she grown up serious, just smiling or nodding at

everything, including jokes in a movie or on television, never laughing?

Her parents didn't laugh either, from what she could remember.

Neither did Steve's parents, come to think of it.

Wow, how sad was that? His parents and her parents never laughed either.

Should she and Steve even think of bringing kids into such a sober, serious family? Kids were supposed to be joyful, live in the moment.

She glanced at the clock on the brand new stove. She had wasted two hours thinking about this. Forty-five minutes from now Steve would be heading out for his normal lunch.

She needed to talk with him. She needed to break the schedule for once and get this out of her head so she could get back to work.

Thirty minutes later his assistant buzzed her into his office.

It was a wonderful office, comfortable and large, with a big oak desk with a high-backed chair Steve had had custom ordered. There was a soft-looking brown cloth couch against one wall and two chairs facing the couch across an oak coffee table.

He looked up and smiled, clearly glad to see her.

Damn he had a handsome smile, one that she had loved since the first time she had seen it.

Then a frown crossed his face and he stood and came around his desk. "What's wrong?"

"Actually nothing, really," she said, kissing him and smiling. "Just needed to talk with my husband about something."

His worried look faded slightly and he indicated they should sit on the couch.

After they sat down, she faced him. "I read an article about how laughing is healthy for a person."

He nodded, the serious look on his face, his dark eyes, looking at her, which meant he was completely focused on her, something she always loved that he did for her.

"Go on," he said, nodding.

"I can't remember the last time I laughed," she said.

And then instantly felt silly. How had she let such a stupid article chew into her mind like that?

Steve looked puzzled, then sat back. "Are you unhappy?"

She shook her head emphatically no. "Not with anything. I love you, I love our life, I love my job, I love our house, everything. It's just that the stupid article made me try to remember the last time I had laughed and I just can't."

Steve looked relieved and he smiled. "I can give you an honest answer to this because I noticed it a few years back myself."

"You did?" she asked, stunned. "You noticed I never laughed?"

"I never laugh either," he said, smiling. "Did you notice that?"

"I did," she said. "And our parents don't laugh."

Steve smiled and nodded.

"So give me the honest answer," she said.

"We don't know how," Steve said. "I certainly don't. And that worried me when I realized it, but every time I tried to laugh it came out artificial, like a cross between a donkey baying and a bus's brakes. Horrid sound."

She smiled at that and shook her head. "Now that was funny."

"But you didn't laugh," he said, smiling.

She sat back. Damned if he wasn't right. She flat didn't even know how to laugh, even at a funny joke.

"Our parents don't laugh, so like anything, we were never trained to laugh," Steve said. "And since both of us were trained the same way, neither of us has been able to help the other one learn."

"What are we going to do when we have kids?" she asked, looking into the dark eyes of the man she loved.

"We'll do the best we can," he said, smiling. "Maybe they can teach us how to laugh? Who knows?"

She stood and he stood and she hugged him, feeling so much better and loving him all the more.

Then she stood back and looked him in the eyes. "Your assistant headed to lunch pretty soon?"

Steve glanced at his watch. "Already gone."

"You have a lunch meeting?" she asked.

"Nothing," he said. "A sandwich across the street at the deli was my big plan.

"Does that door lock?" she asked.

"It does," he said, smiling at her.

"Well get locking, mister," she said, as she started to unbutton her blouse. "Unless you want someone to come in and see your wife naked."

He smiled and moved to the door and locked it.

She was almost naked by the time he got back to her.

"You know," he said, "if you think I'm going to learn to laugh at that beautiful body of yours, you are wrong."

"Not a chance," she said, smiling. "Sex on the office couch is never a laughing matter."

With that, he chuckled and then looked surprised that he had done so spontaneously.

And she chuckled in return at his surprise and felt surprised as well.

"Seems we are making progress," he said, smiling.

"Almost better than an orgasm," she said.

"Not a chance," he said, pushing her back on the couch. "And I'm going to prove that to you right now."

And with that, for the first time in memory, she laughed.

USA *Today* Bestselling Writer

DEAN WESLEY SMITH

A Bryant Street
Story

THE MAN WHO LAUGHED
ON A RAINY NIGHT

THE MAN WHO LAUGHED ON A RAINY NIGHT

Bradford Borne loved rainy, April nights.

He loved to move the body of his dead wife on rainy April nights every year.

He loved how the rain hid his work, covered his tracks, protected him.

But on Bryant Street, even a simple task like moving a body becomes twisted.

———

Bradford Borne stood in the Oregon rain in front of his three-bedroom ranch-style home in the suburbs of Portland. On his right was the flowering plum tree his wife Radella had planted fifteen years before, the year before she died.

Actually, he had planted it on her insistence. She had sat in a lawn chair eating chips while he had done the work.

But now, to protect against the rain, he wore his dark raincoat and a wide-brimmed rain hat, rain pants over his normal tan slacks, and shoe protectors over his brown leather dress shoes. The rain didn't even touch his glasses. He was completely protected from the storm and the chill evening air of late April.

The homes along Bryant Street were silent in the late hours, the blinds pulled on every home, the televisions flickering light to dark and then light again, shadows projected against the windows indicating all his neighbors were in their normal evening zombie state.

The rain also made seeing very far difficult, so he was convinced no one would see him at all. And this time of night on a weeknight, most every one of his neighbors was home in routine. No chance a stray car would pass by tonight.

And the sound of the rain would cover and dampen any sounds he happened to make.

A perfect night to move his dead wife Radella.

Soft ground from the spring rains, no one to see him.

Perfect. Just perfect.

This would be the tenth or maybe eleventh time he had moved Radella in fifteen years. He sometimes couldn't remember.

The first time was because of a sewer issue with the city. Two years after he had buried her the first time, the city needed to run a sewer line to get everyone in the subdivision off their septic tanks. To connect to his home, the new sewer line would run right through where he had buried Radella.

So he dug her up one rainy, muddy night, dealt with the mess, and moved her to the other side of the garage. It had been a long and horrid night.

But as the months went by after that night, he realized he had actually enjoyed the task. He had enjoyed the fear of getting caught, the physical stress and the labor. It had made him feel alive again, something he hadn't felt since the first year of marriage to Radella.

And since the night he had buried her in the first place.

So the following year, again in April, he moved her again, this time to the back corner of his fenced-in backyard, making sure he left no signs at all of anything being disturbed.

He felt so alive after that second time that he ended up meeting a new love of his life.

The official story was that Radella had left, gone back east. He had filed for divorce and faked her signature and was free of her legally. No one really asked about her.

So he married Marilyn that fall and by April Marilyn was going the same way as Radella had gone. Eating, not interested in much of anything but television, yelling at him for every little slight or misstep.

In six months after their marriage, he had become her house slave, the short little man who went to work, earned the money, and then waited on her when he got home.

In late April of that first year of his marriage to Marilyn, she took a five-day trip back to Florida to visit family and he took the opportunity to move Radella again, giving himself that new feeling of life.

By the following April he was almost dead again, his emotions shut down, his caring for life gone.

So on a dark, rainy April night, as Marilyn slept, he smothered her with a plastic bag and buried her in the yard.

He didn't bury her close to Radella. It was a very large backyard with a high wooden fence around it all. Lots and lots of room back there.

Then, when Marilyn's family in Florida asked about her a month later, Bradford had said she had left him with a man named Roger and he knew she was planning on driving to Florida. They didn't seem surprised and said they had never understood what he had seen in her.

He had filed divorce papers and forged her name and they never found her.

And again, no one really ever asked about her. He clearly made poor choices when it came to love.

Or maybe the choice was to marry someone just like that. He could never figure that out.

In late April of that same year, he moved Radella again, trying his best to get some feeling and zest back.

It worked.

So every April, like celebrating an anniversary, he moved Radella one rainy night and Marilyn another.

Neither Marilyn nor Radella had been a light woman on the days of their deaths. Radella had topped over three hundred pounds without clothes and Marilyn had been close to that. Now after all the years wrapped in plastic and tarps, neither woman had gotten lighter.

And Bradford hadn't gotten any younger or stronger.

Bradford was a tiny man by anyone's standards. He owned and ran his own small grocery store just one mile from his home and he had met both Radella and Marilyn when they were still thin.

Radella's death had been different from Marilyn's. He hadn't actually killed her. Not exactly, anyway. One day, as he was serving Radella dinner, she choked on a large bite of steak, medium rare as she liked it, and he sat and watched her die. He didn't feel guilty or sad or anything. In four years she had killed any part of him that showed that kind of emotion.

So he had wrapped her in a large plastic sheet, securing both ends completely. Then wrapped her in another plastic sheet and secured it solidly as well. That evening, actually, was the most he had touched her since their honeymoon.

He left her the next day in the pantry and bought a very heavy tarp and brought it home with him that night. He wrapped her in that and tied it securely with rope.

That night it rained and the digging was easy, and it made him feel alive but he didn't notice until he had had to move her because of the sewer problem.

Now it was April again. It was a dark, rainy night. It was time.

He laughed and took one more look up and down the deserted street. Tonight he would move them both on the same night. How much fun would that be?

He got his shovel and went to where he had buried Radella last year and started to dig, carefully cutting away the sod so he could replace it later. His plan was to move Radella to the back side of the house near the back deck, then move Marilyn into the hole Radella had spent a year in.

He had a tarp beside the hole for the dirt and the rain splattering on the tarp was almost hypnotic.

He was paying no attention at all, just enjoying the feeling of the work and the rain when he suddenly realized he was too deep.

Radella wasn't here.

He was sure he had buried her right there last April. But she wasn't there and a very dead, very heavy woman wrapped in plastic and a tarp didn't just vanish.

He stopped and walked around the large backyard. In fifteen years she had been in eleven places. Or was that just ten. He was getting confused clearly on where in the large backyard she was.

Ahh, well, he would at least move Marilyn tonight.

He finished preparing the hole he had dug, then went over to the end of the wooden fence to the left of his home, near his bedroom window, and started digging, again putting the sod carefully aside and the dirt on another tarp.

And again he got too deep.

Marilyn wasn't there.

For a moment he felt panic, something he hadn't felt in decades. How could he forget where he buried both of his wives?

He once again walked around the backyard trying to jog his memory from last April.

Or was that the April before?

All the Aprils seemed to run together. Had he not been able to find them last April either?

Finally he went and sat in the rain on his back step, letting the water running off his hat calm him.

Then, after a few minutes, he just started to laugh.

Both ex-wives lost. They were here somewhere, he was sure of that, but where was the question.

He sat and just laughed as the rain poured over him, clearing the air, softening the ground, making it a perfect night.

He honestly didn't need to know this year where they were. Next April he would try again to see if he could find them.

Laughing to himself, he went back to work filling in both holes, patting down the sod, cleaning up what dirt had gotten off the tarp by hosing down the lawn in the rain.

When he was all done, you almost couldn't tell any work had been done in those two areas and the rain was starting to ease just slightly.

He cleaned and put away his shovel, cleaned off the tarps and hung them to dry in his tool shed. Then he went in his back door and took off his rain gear.

He felt tired, but alive.

Very much alive.

Alive enough to get through another year.

He started a pot of coffee and stood in the window and watched the rain while it brewed, smiling to himself.

Next April he would find them.

And move them both.

They were out there somewhere.

He was sure of that.

And that was all that mattered.

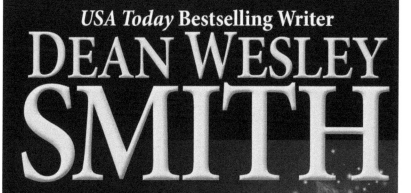

USA *Today* Bestselling Writer

DEAN WESLEY SMITH

When Cleaning
the Garage,
Information Happens

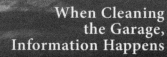

WHY DELAY?
JUST RUB

WHY DELAY? JUST RUB
A BRYANT STREET STORY

Weird things happen on Bryant Street. Even when cleaning a double-car garage.

Late spring, very little sports on television, weather threatening to rain so no golf for Jack. Time to clean out the garage.

Also time to find the old lamp in a pile of garbage. Of course, Jack rubs the lamp to try to clean it.

And on Bryant Street, that means the entire chore of cleaning out a garage snaps into strangeness.

A twisted tale of a man, a wife, and a dirty garage as only can be told on Bryant Street.

———

Jack had finally, after a year of promising and far, far too much gentle nagging and reminders from Connie, his wife, agreed to clean out the garage.

The June day was dark and overcast, threatening rain. Not a day he wanted to be on the golf course anyway. And June sports sucked on television.

Really sucked unless you loved baseball.

So cleaning out the ten years of accumulation and dirt and dust in the large two-car garage finally hit the top of the priority list just because there was nothing better to do.

Nothing.

Absolutely nothing.

And it would buy him some husband points in the great game of marriage.

Jack thought of himself as an average man in the scheme of things. He didn't much mind that. He had started his own accounting firm that now had two offices and five accountants working for him. So he was a successful average guy.

He kept himself in moderate shape for forty years old, with only a small gut and a slight balding spot on the top of his head. He mostly kept himself in shape by walking on nice days from his office to lunch and then on the golf course on weekends. Plus Connie was a sensible cook so he didn't overeat.

Jack actually never did much of anything in excess. Excess was just not his style.

He didn't smoke and drank very little and then only socially and on weekends.

And had been married to Connie since college and had never even thought of straying with another woman.

He had the best woman in the world as a partner, why would he?

They had two kids in college now, both staying in their respective schools during the summer to work part-time jobs instead of coming home. Both had promised they would be home for the 4th of July, which had always been a big deal for Jack. He liked the patriotism and the fireworks, although he wouldn't allow his kids to ever have any fireworks. Just too dangerous.

Connie, his wife, still looked stunning at forty. She was thin, with short brown hair and a wide smile that people liked. She was the funny one of the two of them. The one with the sense of humor; the one that people liked to talk to.

She could charm a group of people in minutes.

She went to the gym every day during the week and owned her own clothing store in the local mall that was doing very well. She had been talking with him about opening a second store and he could see no reason why not.

To Jack, Connie was the dream girl of his life, always had been, always would be. He had no idea why she stayed with him, but she seemed to like their quiet life and routine.

Sometimes he worried about that. Worried about her being with him. But only sometimes.

Again, he never did anything to excess, including worry.

When he had finally agreed to clean out the garage, Connie was excited. She had bought extra trashcans for the job and a lot of extra big black trash bags as well. Plus a number of spray cleaners and a box of rags usually used when painting.

Jack was fairly certain that the garage wasn't that dirty or had that much trash in it. But he never complained when Connie over-prepared for anything. It was one of the many things he loved about her.

He opened both doors to the wide driveway. They had a large four bedroom, three-bath home in a nice subdivision not too far from downtown. He drove a blue SUV and Connie drove a green minivan. Both cars were sitting in their normal parking spaces on the driveway. Neither of their cars had seen the inside of the garage in five years.

Maybe it was past time to do this chore.

The neighborhood looked quiet for a summer Saturday afternoon and the sky had darkened. The air had a calm, muggy feel about it and if he had been a betting man, which he was not, he would bet the predicted rain wasn't far off.

Connie had put on a long white apron over her slacks and white blouse and had slipped on an old pair of running shoes. She pointed to an area beside the garage. "We'll stack the trash there and I'll have it picked up next week."

"A good idea," he said, looking at the piles of stuff for the first time in years with actual natural light on the subject. Where had they gotten all this crap?

More than likely much of it was from the kids.

"We put the stuff still good enough to donate here when we get a spot big enough," Connie said, pointing to a spot near one garage door on her car's side. "I'll have someone come to pick it up next week as well.

"Perfect," he said.

She handed him a pair of work gloves and then pulled on a pair herself.

"This is going to be fun," she said.

That he was convinced would not happen, but it would get done. And that would free up a bunch of time on nice weekends for golf.

They both started on the same pile, mostly pulling items that they both knew were trash and bagging it. And he had been right, most of the trash was from the kids. Leftover parts of their lives that now he and Connie were just bagging and tossing to the curb.

Interesting how that happened with children.

And then, when he and Connie were gone, the kids would come in and toss their lives to the curb. The cycle of things.

After a while, he and Connie had a spot cleared enough to start stacking some items that looked like they could be good enough to donate to a local charity. If it ended up being enough, it would be a nice tax deduction.

If nothing else, he was always the accountant.

Two old kids' bikes started that pile. Then a box of dishes from their first apartment. Opening that box had made them both laugh. The dishes had the worst flower patterns on them that he had ever seen. He had hated those dishes and thought they had vanished a decade ago.

Well, now they would be gone.

Then he found a half-molded old cardboard box and opened it.

Inside was a stack of old pans, some strange metal figures, and an old metal lamp. It looked like it was copper, dented and tarnished, and had the shape of a lamp from India.

"Where did this come from?" he asked, pulling out the lamp and holding it up. It seemed empty and there wasn't a wick in the spout end.

Connie shook her head and came over closer to look. "Not a clue," she said. "More than likely something one of the kids found and brought home for some reason. Maybe as a prop in one of their plays."

He nodded. That made sense. Both his kids had done plays all the way through high school. Costumes and props were always coming home with them.

He was about to toss the beat-up old lamp on the charity pile when some printing on one side caught his eye.

He rubbed off the dirt to see what it said and damned if smoke didn't come from the top of the old lamp, everything froze around him, and a tall guy with some sort of turban on his head appeared out of the smoke. The guy wore big, baggy pants and had on no shirt.

And wow, did he have some muscles.

"Wow, nifty prop," Jack said. "Connie, take a look at this."

When he glanced over, she was frozen in place, a hand reaching for something in the pile, her face smudged with some dirt.

Jack glanced back at the tall guy with his arms crossed like a Mr. Clean commercial standing in his garage.

The guy looked real.

How bad of a cliché was this?

"Connie, nice joke!" Jack said, turning back to her.

She hadn't moved. No one, even in good shape, could hold the position she was in for more than a few seconds.

"Who are you?" Jack asked the big, impossible man standing in his Saturday cleanup project.

The man pointed at the lamp still in Jack's hand.

Jack glanced down at the lamp. On the side the words read, "Rub me once for the Genie to appear, rub me twice to get a wish."

Jack quickly set the lamp down and went over to Connie. She was still in the same position.

He moved her arm in closer to her body. He could move her just fine, so he went into the kitchen, got a chair and brought it out and worked her around until she was sitting down.

The guy was still standing in the garage, his arms crossed over his bare chest.

Jack went back inside and tried to call the police, but all the lines were dead. Nothing at all was working.

Everything was frozen.

He went back out to the guy and just stared at the hunk of man.

He flat didn't believe the guy was a genie, but he was going to play along with the gag until someone started laughing.

"Can you talk to me, answer questions?"

The man did not move. He just kept staring straight

ahead like there was something real important on the garage wall.

Connie kept sitting on the chair. She hadn't moved at all.

Jack went out to look up and down the street and that was when he saw a few raindrops just hanging in the air.

Time had really stopped around this guy.

Oh, shit!

How was this possible?

Genies in lamps didn't exist in American suburbia. They existed in old fairytales and kids' books.

Jack reached up and touched one drop of water with a finger. It didn't move.

And nothing was supporting it.

"Shit! Shit! Shit!"

Jack seldom swore, even on the golf course, but he figured this time if any was appropriate.

He moved back around the big man with the cloth on his head and carefully picked up the lamp.

Nothing had changed.

And there was no writing on the other side or on the bottom of the old thing.

He set the lamp down carefully on the concrete garage floor and went back into the house to get a glass of water and try to think.

Of course, the water wouldn't come out of the tap and he couldn't get the fridge open.

He was going to have to rub that stupid lamp to get this to end.

But none of this could be happening. Magic wasn't real. This had to be an illusion of some sort.

But if it was real, what should he wish for? He had seen enough bad movies and bad cartoons to know that wishes from genies never turned out as well as hoped.

He sat down at the kitchen table and looked around the house. What would he wish for? He had a beautiful wife he loved, a great home, enough money.

And if he said he wished for nothing, that might be how he ended up.

So he had to be careful. If this was real, which it seemed to be, he needed to ask for something innocent.

But what?

What did he really want?

He could ask for a better golf game, but he wouldn't feel right about that because the fun of golf was in the chase, not just suddenly, magically being better.

He flat couldn't think of anything.

He stood and went back out into the large garage.

Connie was still sitting in the position he had left her. She looked even more beautiful than before, even with the smudge on her cheek.

He had no idea why she stayed with him.

And then he realized that question had been bothering him for a long, long time. They had a comfortable relation-ship, based on family and familiarity and habit.

Was he nothing more than a habit to her?

He finally had the chance to know.

He picked up the lamp, then carefully thought through his question and rubbed the lamp solidly.

The genie's large dark eyes focused on Jack.

"Your wish?"

"I do not understand why Connie, my wife, has stayed with me for all these years. I would like to know if she has ever had an affair with another man or woman while we have been married?"

"No," the genie said. "She has not."

Then the genie laughed, a sound that Jack was certain might break a few windows if it got louder.

As smoke started to come from the lamp and swirl around the genie, the big man shook his head. "You two really need to get a life. And that's coming from a guy who lives in an old lamp."

"Why?" Jack asked.

The genie shook his head. "She asked the exact same thing about you."

"She did?"

The genie laughed again. "She doesn't understand why you have stayed with her all these years either. Try talking more, would you?"

Then he was gone.

And so was the memory of the genie being there.

Outside the garage door, the rain was just starting to fall.

"What am I doing sitting down?" Connie asked, looking around.

Jack had no idea. He just tossed the lamp into the charity pile and went to her.

"I ever tell you how beautiful you are?" he said as she sat there, looking very stunned.

She laughed and stood. "Nice try, mister. How did I get sitting there on one of our good kitchen chairs?"

"Don't ask me why you are lounging around," he said. "I've been sorting through junk."

He kissed her and turned back to the shrinking pile. It would be nice to get his car back in here again. He had to admit that.

And besides, on a rainy summer afternoon, what better thing was there to do than spend the day with the love of his life, no matter what he was doing.

A big, booming voice inside Jack's head said, *"Now that's better."*

Then Jack thought he heard a laugh, but it was actually only thunder in the distance.

NEWSLETTER SIGN-UP

Follow Dean on BookBub

Be the first to know!
Just sign up for the Dean Wesley Smith newsletter, and keep up with the latest news, releases and so much more—even the occasional giveaway.

So, what are you waiting for? To sign up go to deanwesleysmith.com.

But wait! There's more. Sign up for the WMG Publishing newsletter, too, and get the latest news and releases from all of the WMG authors and lines, including Kristine Kathryn Rusch, Kristine Grayson, Kris Nelscott, *Pulphouse Fiction Magazine, Smith's Monthly,* and so much more.
To sign up go to wmgpublishing.com.

ABOUT THE AUTHOR
DEAN WESLEY SMITH

Considered one of the most prolific writers working in modern fiction, with more than 30 million books sold, *USA Today* bestselling writer Dean Wesley Smith published far more than a hundred novels in forty years, and hundreds of short stories across many genres.

At the moment he produces novels in several major series, including the time travel Thunder Mountain novels set in the Old West, the galaxy-spanning Seeders Universe series, the urban fantasy Ghost of a Chance series, a super-hero series starring Poker Boy, and a mystery series featuring the retired detectives of the Cold Poker Gang.

His monthly magazine, *Smith's Monthly*, which consists of only his own fiction, premiered in October 2013 and offers readers more than 70,000 words per issue, including a new and original novel every month.

During his career, Dean also wrote a couple dozen *Star Trek* novels, the only two original *Men in Black* novels, Spider-Man and X-Men novels, plus novels set in gaming and television worlds. Writing with his wife Kristine Kathryn Rusch under the name Kathryn Wesley, he wrote the novel for the NBC miniseries The Tenth Kingdom and other books for *Hallmark Hall of Fame* movies.

He wrote novels under dozens of pen names in the worlds of comic books and movies, including novelizations of almost a dozen films, from *The Final Fantasy* to *Steel* to *Rundown*.

Dean also worked as a fiction editor off and on, starting at Pulphouse Publishing, then at *VB Tech Journal*, then Pocket Books, and now at WMG Publishing, where he and Kristine Kathryn Rusch serve as series editors for the acclaimed *Fiction River* anthology series.

For more information about Dean's books and ongoing projects, please visit his website at www.deanwesley-smith.com and sign up for his newsletter.

For more information:
www.deanwesleysmith.com

f facebook.com / deanwsmith3
P patreon.com / deanwesleysmith
BB bookbub.com / authors / dean-wesley-smith

Milton Keynes UK
Ingram Content Group UK Ltd.
UKHW011835160724
445364UK00010B/114/J